Bastard Heart

The Gerald Cable Book Award Series

Love Fugue
Shulamith Wechter Caine

Sleeping Upside Down
Kate Lynn Hibbard

Dime Store Erotics
Ann Townsend

What Kills What Kills Us
Kurt S. Olsson

Bodies that Hum
Beth Gylys

The Odds of Being
Daneen Wardrop

Inventing Difficulty
Jessica Greenbaum

Blue to Fill the Empty Heaven
Joel Friederich

Why They Grow Wings
Nin Andrews

Best Western and Other Poems
Eric Gudas

Odd Botany
Thorpe Moeckel

The Lessons
Joanne Diaz

A Parade of Hands
James Hoch

Close By
Gigi Marks

Lime
Audrey Bohanan

The Invented Child
Margaret Mackinnon

Any Holy City
Mark Conway

Bastard Heart

Raphael Dagold

Silverfish Review Press
Eugene, Oregon

Acknowledgments

Grateful acknowledgement is given to the editors of the following journals in which these poems first appeared, some in earlier versions:

Western Humanities Review: "Voltage," "Learning to Eat Apples," and "Catalogue: Butcher's Hill, Baltimore, Summer 1988." *Quarterly West*: "Season of Burning Leaves." *Northwest Review*: "Spinoza." *two girls review*: "Bastard Heart" and "Fixing." *Bridges: A Journal for Jewish Feminists and Our Friends*: "For Whom." *Clackamas Literary Review*: "Seeing My Wife at the Whitney" and "Getting on a Horse." *Perceptions: A Magazine of the Arts*: "Poppies in Provence," "Bending Glass," and "You Want Something More I Want Something Different." *Shirim: a Jewish Poetry Journal*: "Collections" and "New Elements." *Indiana Review*: "Radio Tuning." *Born*: "Tree Heart." *Frank: An International Journal of Contemporary Writing and Art*: "Dirt Heart."

Cover photo: *C. pulsum* (from the series, *Cors mortali*) © 2005 by Dianne Kornberg

Kurt S. Olsson was the 2012 GCBA final judge.

Published by
Silverfish Review Press
PO Box 3541
Eugene, OR 97403
www.silverfishreviewpress.com

Distributed by
Small Press Distribution
800-869-7553
spd@spdbooks.org
www.spdbooks.org

Library of Congress Cataloging-in-Publication Data

Dagold, Raphael.
  Bastard heart / Raphael Dagold. -- First edition.
    pages cm
  ISBN 978-1-878851-64-2
  I. Title.
  PS3604.A332545B37 2014
  813'.6--dc23
                              2013038154

9 8 7 6 5 4 3 2 First Printing
Printed in the United States of America

Contents

Season of Burning Leaves   9

Learning to Eat Apples   11

For Whom   13

Spinoza   14

Catalogue: Butcher's Hill, Baltimore, Summer 1988   16

Parts Unknown   17

Seeing My Wife at the Whitney   19

Bastard Heart   20

Bending Glass   21

In the Woods   23

Like to Need   25

In the Field   27

Voltage   29

Collections   30

January 1995   33

In Manhattan, After   35

Fixing   38

You Want Something More I Want Something Different   39

My Mother Jumps Out of a Boat   40

Radio Tuning   42

New Elements   44

Tattoo   46

Tree Heart   47

Getting on a Horse   49

Rising   50

Wild Flies   52

The Crowd   54

Collapsing Frame   55

Poppies in Provence   57

Insulin   58

At a Window, Wide to September   59

End of May, Leaving   60

June, a New House   61

July, Hungry   62

Fireworks   63

Dirt Heart   66

Bastard Heart

Season of Burning Leaves

He is looking for something perfect
in the vacant lot full of voices.

We are knives made of a diamond,
say shards of plate glass edged like water
beside dead crowns of August goldenrod.

I am as big as your head,
nods the dull rock squatting
like a dumb frog in the glass.

I am still perfect, says a half marble
bedded in dirt. *What isn't?*

Halved, quartered, split in a hundred
sharpnesses each with its own whole summer
glittering, as from the articulated eyes
of the green fly shining like gasoline in oil,
each perfect thing:

there's the imagined part, mythic,
library book driven, whole beings
popping from one milky solidity

into the next, face of a pomegranate,
face of a leopard, face of a dove's tail,
face of the chain-link fence
with a hole at the level of his knee,
face in the forearm of his fake leather jacket
where a broken girl put out her cigarette

ten times slow. Face out of black holes.
But August again evaporates
into particles of something else,
a whole head out of the lot:
ears of a rusted hinge,
brow of a broken wheel,

throat out of glass and cracked rubber,
nape of a Nike sole,
skull of the frog stone, eyes,

eyes of the sweet smell
of locust leaves eaten by oxygen.

Let's go, says the head. *Let's go.*

Learning to Eat Apples

My father is driving the blue Ford Falcon,
I'm in the back seat with my brother,
we're on our way to the synagogue
on Sunday morning, we've each had an apple
and wonder what to do with the cores.
Should we, after we've been through the whole sweet
crunch, the skin, the juice mixing its sugary tang
in our mouths, should we know what to do
after the first bite of the whole fruit,
after we've bitten off as much of the last pulp
as we possibly can with our little teeth,
should we know what to do with the cores?
Maybe we should put them in the ashtray, maybe
that's what I say, before our father says
Here, give them to me, I'll eat them.
Maybe our father doesn't really know what to do
either, so he makes gnashing noises as he eats
until the complicated middle is gone inside him,
the plastic-y slivers around the seeds, the seeds
themselves, whole or half chewed, down
to his stomach, where I wonder if they'll grow
a little before he digests them, or if he'll grow
a resistance to the cyanide I know even then
laces apple seeds. He puts the dry stems
in the clean ashtray, and it's fun, our father
being goofy, no one in their right mind
would eat an apple core and like it,
it's from a time before we were born,
the frugal happiness and pleasure in efficiency,
his large fingers bigger than the skinny cores,
his answer to waste simply not to end up with any.
Our mother will pick us up after noon
and take us to her house for the day,
or maybe for the week if regular school has just let out

and we've brought our suitcases,
we'll go with her in to the city and our other life.
Eating apples next time with our father,
he'll know what to do, and the time after that,
he'll pretend that he likes it, his favorite
part, what he wants more than anything.

For Whom

One day, my older brother
took a tennis ball from the cigar box—
one of the places he'd written
I want to kill myself in magic marker—
and led me outside.
He said he'd throw it clear
over the house for me to catch.
The house was small, still
beneath the sudden ball,
my brother's face, I knew, tense,
following the arc until it disappeared.
It has to be okay to wonder
if what you think your life is, isn't it.

I don't want any trouble.
Paralyzed, vague, in a hospital bed
with Guillain-Barré syndrome, my grandmother
after sixty years of perfect English—
whom, she'd correct me, *for whom*—
spoke only Yiddish, lost words
to two men no longer tuned
to hear them—my father, mouth open,
suddenly three again grasping
at language in a Baltimore duplex,
my grandfather, scowling, terrified,
accusing her memory's brief success,
She'll die in a language
we spent our lives getting out of.

He's dead now. She's alive.
The words don't make a choice.
My brother's throw comes over
the horizon. I catch it.
I catch it and catch it.

Spinoza

How many times did he tell me of walking to the civil service exam
down melting sidewalks of Baltimore to get all the questions right,
to finish first and be the only one that day to shine?

A Zionist in vain who searched Israel for his family's holy path,
a path perhaps he saw in the libraries and museums he took his
    children
after a week's work and Saturday morning's call to the synagogue,

he read Spinoza and raised a battered forefinger in his retelling,
a poor ecclesiast to boast in monologue of all he'd gathered
as he put ten rubber bands around a bag of chips and we nodded at
    his words.

And in the last decade of his life he came upon us in our shady
    suburb,
visiting longer than anyone wanted, sneering hurt from our grudges
to sulk away folded in the aluminum lawn chair up from Florida.

I didn't understand the ancient words our Rabbi spoke across the
    cemetery's lawn
any more than I knew why my grandfather had poured ketchup over
    everything he ate,
but I felt those words and cried before standing in line to trowel dirt
    on his coffin:

We are the light of the Lord: We will help you to be on your way:
As he rode the mail train up the northeast corridor organizing zip-
    codes,
the engine and freight cars rushing then screeching down in their
    wind—

what was he thinking when he threw out letter bags onto the train
    platform?
About Spinoza and his many-headed God, about the equity of
    atoms in an arc?
He must have been a completely different person each day by New
    York.

14

Who then is given me? The worker, the philosopher? The pedant,
    the worrier?
He did tell me *Stop your reading and go out,* called me *Absent-minded*
    professor
when I left my crystal radio project out on the kitchen telephone
    table—

yet I'd seen him leaning into the dial plugged into its tinny earphone,
mouth half open, with his furrowed brow and bony nose I have the
    shadow of
tuning in the old world, hearing a new and slighter one.

Catalogue: Butcher's Hill, Baltimore, Summer 1988

Vomit, broken whiskey bottles, half-burned mattresses
      soaked through by firehoses, steaming
      next to a side door in full summer sun;
heaps of discarded sundresses, children's underwear, and videotapes
      puckering with the drying urine of adolescent boys;
alley rats BB-gunned off fire escapes;
costume wigs skewered by splintered broomsticks
      leaning from galvanized trashcans;
waist-high grass stiff in an empty lot,
      unopened tins of refried beans bulging along its path;
a hubcap smashed on the rods of a rusty sewer grate,
      a motorcycle burning ten feet from a stop sign,
      dry dog droppings kicked open,
      spread like small stones across the sidewalk;
girls in smudged dresses heaving bricks at boys behind the chain-link
      around a narrow strip of lawn;
emphatic tracts of liberation papering the windows
      of an abandoned corner store,
      written in a schizophrenic's frantic code;
rowhouse screens painted with bucolic vistas, hiding old women
      watching profane young lovers arm-in-arm at dusk;
cats birthing wet litters in abandoned strollers
      parked at the intersection of two alleys;
iron-gated archways between formstone housefronts,
      cement backyards with console TVs and faded Tonkas;
the drawn-out baritone of an arabber calling out his sweetest choices,
      Georgia peaches, cucumbers, cantaloupes piled on the wagon
      behind his horse and its jingling mane,
      the arabber's calls following Pratt Street's long hill,
      catching on tiny side streets, Castle, Chapel, Durham,
      floating toward tall buildings near the highway overpass,
      the harbor downtown, the small piers
      where nine-year-olds cast their lines for fish.

Parts Unknown

Stranger than metaphor—
the shapes beneath our shapes—
a bird lay downtown at noon,
still, tiny, featherless, its swollen middle
half blue like dawn, like veins
in the crook of my elbow,
and I don't know why—
I guess I could make it up—
why I thought of that bird
after my wife, months before
the wedding, asked how Jews
could be a people, and the people,
a religion, and I, shaking,
suddenly alone, turned again
to books—to read to her,
to both of us, of the diaspora—
the scattering of the Jews
among the gentiles, I read,
outnumbering Jews in Israel
by the 1st century AD . . .
the chief centers have varied,
Spain, France, Germany, Russia . . .
and then diaspora within diaspora,
1290 expulsion from England,
1306 from France, 1492 from Spain,
a people, I said, who spread
because we were shattered,
whose laws bound us
and made us strange in lands
that made us strangers—
1144 medieval blood accusations,
1215 Fourth Lateran Council and yellow badge,
1348 ghettos in Germany, 1516 in Venice,
1391 pogroms in Spain, over and over,

this home, that home, half my own family
to America from Eastern Europe,
that pale of settlement for whose Jews
the Middle Ages ended only in 1917,
and only then, telling this one
brief history, did I begin
to cry, to rock the loss
over, and over, and this woman
before me, blood or stranger,
friend or foe?
Then I didn't know.
I still don't know
about the dead bird,
why on the sidewalk or why here,
why the sun had no shadow there
or why its stomach, blue and taut,
here drew me to my own blood
and my vision of dawn:
except I saw through its smooth body
to all the naked birds,
blind, hungry miracles
and it was that familiar, over and over,
of course on the sidewalk,
of course there was a tree
it fell from,
of course I remembered it
and nothing else,
and of course my wife
here with her face unfolded,
her eyes the color of noon,
of course with the blunt object
of her questions,
this woman I've given my heart,
with her questions she's raised
a tide of saltwater,
my own body's heaving.

Seeing My Wife at the Whitney

Again I'm loving what I can not see, beating
my heart against it, the black thirds

of Steichen's early landscapes,
silver all-the-way dark and the shapes above—

tree limbs, voluptuous clouds, rocks like minor gods—
reflected in each pool of blackness.

I'm working my gaze into platinum, silver,
into gum bichromate, direct carbon

prints which ache, and pierce me.
My wife vibrates on the floor of my brain.

The clouds are intricate mountains
making and unmaking themselves.

A woman whose hair suddenly glistens
waits for me to move so she will not break

my gaze, seeking shapes in murmuring crystals
of platinum, layered dark ground and boundless.

Bastard Heart

The blackbirds are ripping a hole
in the sky. They are like
minnows: a wave swallowing
itself. And a heart. They are a heart,
a hole, a house, where long rents
divide the rooms, a house
that one by one collects
itself among the angled millet,
ruffling shells of bird bodies
in each place among the rooms,
among the heart they've made
themselves into, heart a break in sky
to never close. Why they are collecting
so many black and glistening mouthfuls,
why they place themselves veiled
before fluttering up in another wave,
is anybody's bastard heart to fill a mouth:
they are. And they are turning
wings so thin, invisible between
the gravel and the foothills' sage,
of course they cut the sky
in unpieceable halves, of course
the brain's a heart conjoined
by merest bolts of what
it doesn't understand, of course
the heart turns broadside with its emboldened
windows, its flat glass of old divided
lights, turns flat to whipped wind,
of course the birds' black wings turn
the same wide dark, each the same time
like the unschooled flock,
an open house the heart is.

Bending Glass

It's not the rim, it's the curved plane of the wineglass
I get between my teeth, bite gently, find the right place

and steady pressure so my jaw will flex just as much
as the thin glass can take, as if I were bending a stick

and holding it taut the moment before it snaps, that swoon
where the glass fits my mouth as if it *were* my mouth,

a part gone missing. I'm in the den. Grownups
are all around me, talking up high

with drinks and little plates of food, perched
on chairs laughing, a houseful of voices like low clouds

which gather and dissipate and gather again, a weather
I'm walking through with a wineglass someone thinks

is cute, and which my mother thinks will break inside
my mouth, I'll bite on shards with blood on my lips.

From the kitchen she gives me
hot banana bread with so much butter

and overripe fruit I only take one bite.
A fire lights half the room, logs dropping embers

into the fine dust left by newspaper rolls,
color advertisements gone up in quiet

flames of green and blue inking the heat.
I want the cool glass turning warm in my mouth.

I want a blue flame of ink silent in fire.
The glass breaks. Or it doesn't break. If it breaks

I don't get hurt, I've never split my lip
or swallowed glass. It must not break. I swallow

the possibility like food my body thinks about
for years, *it breaks, it doesn't break.*

In the Woods

In woods between clipped gardens
of Haverford State Hospital for the Mentally Ill

and smooth acres of the retirement community,
on a walk from wedding details

in my future mother-in-law's apartment,
we saw trash stuck in a young birch—

milk cartons driven on the ends of branches,
paper plates, impaled, held up and fluttering,

plastic coke bottles bobbing down low,
foil hung to glitter in the upper leaves,

clean, abundant, some fallen, all faded—
neither frenzied, nor patiently composed:

urgently, maybe, a need from old daydreams,
a gate assembled, safe passage secured.

In Baltimore, we'd seen a guy writing neat unsequenced figures
in his book at a late-night Dunkin' Donuts

where, clumped in groups, were hip young Russian Jews,
older black men talking work and politics,

suburban Jews who'd moved from New York
flirting with the giggly black girl behind the counter,

down-and-out white regulars slumped at their coffee,
and one guy in camouflage muttering *Our country . . . belong. . . .*

At the edge of this amazement, the scribbler bent
at his book, writing fast five-digit columns

without pause, as his friend the dumb-joke teller,
on a walk from his stool, nodded down at the pages

of what? Lottery numbers? Names for tiny spirits?
Who knows? They were notes or emblems, mimicry or genius,

a bridge before him or markers left to keep his way—
all of it. A way to make some sense, to keep himself himself.

Before the tree, the talisman or gate,
old folks' home behind us, nuthouse fence ahead,

our wedding in three days, we marveled
at this eerie shrine, excited, nervous,

some part of that always, even now, unsharable.
My fingers felt a pressure—her hand, mine,

something to clutch, something to yank away from.

Like to Need

In Baltimore, Paul and Jimmy wait on the stoop
with their dime bag of skunky leaf.
They're up under the sodium lights
and the five cop cars have left
after jerking a man against a hood
so he'd let his body, slack, cuffed,
be led away alone.
Paul tells Jimmy about charity and hope,
how everybody's here to help each other,
how Arlene helped him hide
that night he got crazy and cut somebody's eye,
how nobody should push him off their stoop,
how his aunt took him in when he banged her door
drunk again, after somebody's brother
threatened him out the house with Karate
and he said *You know Karate?*
I know KA-RAZY! I know KA-RAAZY!

Listen Jimmy, we gotta love each other
like the winos do, like Jesus.
That guy with the brother kicked me out,
he was my friend. He loaned me money.
He told me a story. He could read.
He had typewriters all over. He was crazy.
He kept his windows open so I borrowed
his leather jacket. Everybody needs
something different. I didn't see him after jail.
But like I told him, You're my friend
because I tell you things. You write
because it's what you like to need.

Jimmy coughs. He lights a cigarette
and he believes. His lungs are black
and they must stay that way.
He looks down the rotting sidewalk

with its junk trees growing up
where rowhouse formstone meets concrete.
Two boys fight barefoot over a Coke
and it's after midnight.
When the bottle breaks,
one cuts his foot and sits down scared.
His friend kneels, pulls out the chip of glass,
then helps the hurt one limp home.

In the Field

I'm in the middle of the school field at recess
with Cheryl Paul, who everyone teases
because they say she's a retard,
and I think maybe she is, she's slow,
but seems older, too, more developed,
and is sad all the time, or nervous.
She's asking me to show her how to fight.
I don't know how to fight, I tell her,
but she says *Yes you do, you're a boy,*
show me something, show me anything.
I've never been in a real fight, though I've
imagined them, especially in third grade, in love
with Miriam, who sat beside me with long hair
and with whom I imagined holding hands,
a crowd of boys following, taunting us,
so I would turn around and run
at the boy in front, then do it again
after walking a few more steps with Miriam.
The only actual fight I've had was with my friend
Michael Chapnek, who is one of the most boring
kids I've ever met. He's boring except he believes
he is the Catcher in the Rye: he has a signature mitt,
he remembers being inside his mother
with his older sister Carol, playing outfield
in high grass of a meadow, and one time
it's his sister who sails over,
he tries but can't reach her, he stretches up,
jumps, calls out telling her not to leave,
she sails past, beyond, out,
and he is left alone floating in the darkness.
One time at school, Michael Chapnek cuts
in front of me lining up to go inside
from recess. *I'm going to get him for that,*
I say to the boy behind me in line.

After school, I go to his house, stand on the walk
a few yards from the front steps, call out
for him to come and play.
As soon as he reaches me, I attack him,
I grab his arm and pull, reach around his chest,
try to wrestle him down. As we struggle,
Michael's sister Carol rushes out,
pins me to her from behind,
she's a teenager and almost as big as our parents.
She scolds me and tells me to stop.
I laugh, I say she sounds just like my mother,
an insult, because all of us really are kids.
I say I'll stop, and as soon as she lets me go,
I run at Michael, knock him down, then leave.
In the field with Cheryl, the grass just mowed,
the midday light evenly around us, I show her
something, some move, that puts her down
prone, on her back, gently, her eyes closed.
I know the surface of the field smells
like roots of clover and clumps of tan grass
from the big mower ridden by the gym teacher,
that the smell of bark and oak leaves
doesn't reach us from the backyard trees
shielding houses on two sides of the field,
that the empty playground tastes like metal
and feels like sand. When I look up,
I see what Cheryl has seen, three boys
walking towards us, they must have been watching,
we both know what they're thinking.
Lie down, Cheryl whispers, *just lie down*
and close your eyes, and pretend you don't see them.

Voltage

"The best image to sum up the unconscious is Baltimore in the early morning."
                                                        Jacques Lacan

Aaron believes he can send voltage
with lantern batteries hooked in series

through the air to his balsa airplane.
It'll fly across his room, even beyond,

as far as the small harbor where we talk,
bumming around on cobblestones, looking

for cigarette butts with enough tobacco
left for Aaron to smoke. In the middle distance,

a tug pulls a trash barge, gulls squalling
over the heap. Nearer, almost close enough

to touch, the red-painted shark mouth
of the USS Torsk gleams its jagged teeth

toward Broadway Market, its produce stands,
fishmongers, greasy dives. Aaron again explains

his theory of voltage, how #14 bellwire
from Sam and Delbert's Variety is perfect

for the popsicle-stick windings.
The unlit skeleton of the Domino Sugar neon

traces itself against the blue sky across the harbor.
Down the block, pigeons light

on the Angel Tavern's sign, marking
its wooden wings with white dirt.

Collections

Why do I look up? But there they are,
hundreds of ladybugs on the ninth-floor stairwell's ceiling
in this building where, three days ago, a student jumped
after flicking the last of her cigarette's ashes in the can.

The ladybugs, in from the dazzle of the tame trees' canopy,
are like fish eggs on a capsized hull—
everything's turned but gravity,
insects children wish on above me calm as flesh,
my footfalls clicking up into my ears
as if these offices were sharply cracking,
casement windows flapping open like the sudden shudder
of my body in an unremembered dream last night,
the student's body falling story by story like nothing

I have seen. I didn't see it.
I heard she was Asian. And then Jewish.
I heard she lifted up her arms like Jesus in the moment of decision.
And that it must have been the pressure, the quiet push
of what? Over the edge? Excellence? Success?

2.

No figures now. Stories:

In my synagogue one year,
we children tried collecting bottle caps:
six million, each to represent a murdered Jew.
We counted and bagged them each Sunday,
learning how hard it is to gather
six million anything, however small and insignificant,
however different from us and ubiquitous.

The mounds of caps did recall mass graves—
not graves—big ditches—
to which, before the building of the ovens,
the dead were carted
and thrown in askew like branches—
not branches—like human bodies in a ditch,
piles I saw in photographs each year I was a child.

Some kids, I thought, were cheating
when their fathers, pharmacists,
brought in Glad bags full of plastic caps:
Merrill-Dow, Parke-Davis, Upjohn—
perverse, too, bringing medicine to the dead.
Did we get six million? Even half? Success?

3.

1911, New York. Yes, the Lower East Side.

The sea-swell of immigrants, a third of Eastern Europe's Jews,
has squeezed itself from tenements crowded with bodies and cloth, up,
up into factories crowded with bodies and cloth,

women working faster, faster, rows of machines fed bolts of cotton,
flywheels slick with sweat, the heat, fingertips, the pressure,
an atom slips, a spark, a flame, a blaze, the building's blazing

eleven floors up. The fire pushes harder, hard against workers
with a lurid choice as, too far below, the firemen and gathered crowd
crane their necks or bob and weep. The workers choose, and many
        jump,

each one another of one hundred seventy-five that day to mourn for.
One man, courteous before he leaps, helps women to a window ledge:
Habit, power? Mercy, beauty? How does he choose?

The tired, the poor, the ashes-to-ashes.
In Auschwitz, no windows high enough to die from.
In the vaults, no windows. Above, a smokestack echoing fallout.

January 1995

For weeks they've bombed the capital, for weeks
I've hesitated writing of the face
on television more like mine
than any I have seen outside my family.
In synagogue, when there were reasons
for us—my brother, my father, uncle, grandfather—
reasons to be together for a family
blessing, a Bar Mitzvah, a prayer,
congregants would come and say,
What are you, clones? we looked to them
so much alike. The Chechen fighter,
filmed this morning, enters the circle dance,
gun slung to his back—bodies rocking
backward, forward, a chant, the stamp
of right feet pushing the circle closer,
the press of torsos, arms, shouts
one shape Islam has taken, strange,
familiar—they say, *we will die here*
or take it to the mountains, already
they've fought past hope,
impossibly continuing a 300-year fight—
what our president is calling
an *internal problem*. For years I've felt,
in the city where I was born, spirits
passing through me, through low buildings
flanked by skyscrapers, through streets
now run with buses. This has nothing
to do with flesh, has everything
to do with blood. They must have fled
the threat of soldiers, these spirits,
my great-grandparents arriving from pogroms
of the old world to the bewilderment of the new,
they must have given me this vision of a Grozny cousin
whose throat seems to speak the diaries

I've read, Passover through May 1943,
of the Warsaw Ghetto Uprising fought
in isolation—pistols, bottles of gasoline,
no retreat plan, hundreds of bunkers
defiant for weeks, more, against tanks,
machine guns, poison gas—
while outside, the city watched flames
from balconies. Our president is right.
It is an *internal problem*, ours, teeming in our cities.

In Manhattan, After

Like Hiroshima's vague
silhouettes of stunned
bodies blinded, seared
photographically, negatives
hurled by heat and light
onto still walls of bank
buildings far enough the shock
of the blast, a sun's rumble,
left them standing in the other
shock, the light, the instant
of exposure x-rayed blindly
making flat surprised doubles
of suits, dresses, carefully
arranged hair; and like
the hollows left by ash,
hot, soft, poisonous
around the people of Pompeii,
after nineteen centuries filled
with plaster, making casts
of elbows, fingers, eyes
reaching from their absence
to tell us they were human—
in New York it is like this,
an afterimage across the street
from where the two towers stood,
this small stone church's
graveyard where Alexander Hamilton
is buried, carved markers
untouched, as if they'd breathed
in each body from the whole
skyward block forty feet
away, as if they could
do that, distilled versions,
sitting with upright shoulders

in dirt the same dirt
under all the buildings, under
sidewalks where people mill,
stand close, stroll, even, try
to understand, wearing
black baseball caps and winter
watchcaps with white letters
reading FDNY and GROUND ZERO,
they are looking up
into the middle distance,
trying to see what can't be
seen in bright sun of a Sunday,
their backs turned to the graveyard,
the light softer there, under
trees, an old light humming
on the grey stones,
they are taking pictures of the air,
as I am, of the absence,
taking pictures of people taking
pictures of the absence
of the buildings, the sun
behind a black, shrouded
office building casting
a shadow where no shadow
has fallen to ground for decades,
and I wish—as a child
sometimes hopes to be transported
to a different life, to flash
from one life to another
life—I wish that they,
on the 105th, the 79th, floors
had indeed travelled in the clear
sunlight down and become
the untouched weathered marks
of another century's hope
for remembrance, for voyage
into an uncluttered, a bright

future, no murk
of killing, jet fuel, red
revenge, distant lack
of honor or sense, caves
of hatred, desks of targets,
operational theaters of metal,
horses, money, and blood.

Fixing

Where I'd like to be is in the fumes of gasoline
with wrenches placed like scalpels on a clean rag,
tearing my bike's cylinders down past the pushrods
until I got past it all to the engine block
and could insert an extra gasket to relieve the high compression.
That's what my boot smells like right now, like gasoline,
because my right-hand carb still drips
and where I'd like to be is adjusting the float
so the needle stops the flow as it's supposed to.
Isn't it odd how everything would be perfect then,
a road would open up and smell like pine needles,
there'd be a bend in the road at the top of a hill like nothing
I have ever seen or ever will again
and isn't it odd, at times like these, how cigarettes
are rolled in desperate measure to the creaking of a chair?
You don't know where I am
and I won't tell you. I'll tell you this:
last night I couldn't speak
or breathe, I woke and couldn't say a word
but whimpered like a human being
who'd lost his speech and couldn't name it.
It didn't last long, but what's inside us
pilloried and small in heart valves, up spinal nerves
to the head with its cranial veins and then sinus cavities
to pressure us so it can't open and it can't open?

You Want Something More
I Want Something Different

We are in an ocean   like an ocean the swells
well up between us and   subside to a flatness the floor
flat like the floor without weight   without height
yes you are completely   responsible for me for what
I am I am frustrated I am going   into the hallway
because I am so angry   I am not stopping this I am
a tide between us like a tide   turning we have made
enough for us, turn against   each other you are striding
toward me I am sitting the swell   flattens to nothing
we take our hands   to each other my fingers
across your mouth the flat   of your hand cuffing
the side of my face   above my cheekbone we back
away we hate each other a minute   a hot buzz we are
not children   this is unlike our cats swats
at each other forgotten   when one of them turns
away, we have not turned   as I write this claiming
us claiming we are closer   than we have ever been.

My Mother Jumps Out of a Boat

She jumps at the word "down," as in, *sit the fuck down,*
and she's out into the cold bay, past midnight, past drinking,

past music, pay-phone calls, waiting on barstools and being stood up,
she is sixty and listens to her heart throbbing under

her clothes, under her ribs, she is saying she waited,
she went to one crowded bar and then another, thinking the jazz

band John said he'd drive up from the shore to see with her
that night, late, eleven, already late, she'd walked the whole way down

the hill to meet him in the clear moonlight and maybe—
thinking maybe she'd got the place wrong, was it *The Cat's Eye,*

or *The Wharf Rat,* or *The Horse You Came In On,* or the time, the
    wrong
time. Or maybe John had an accident, a car crash, cut

his thumb with a skilsaw working on a roof, or just working late, or
maybe practicing his sax with an old friend who has voluptuous

hair as hers once was, down to her waist like the petite
laughing girls John was always looking at before they danced.

Her hair is like the ocean still shaking on the corrugated
sand of a broad beach, thrown down from a swell

with its origins where sea creatures live in impossible pressure, blind.
She waited and what she wanted was a romantic walk in the full

moon's light, the light that means to her the world will change
or is full of all the power to change, then in the full moon a ride

on John's boat from the harbor, the oars, this idyll, this twining,
she's telling him, her heart a swell and its undertow both, shaking.

On the boat they've finally got to together, late, a chance
meeting by the water after last call, finally he'd shown up,

as she's telling her heart on the water he tells her *sit the fuck
down*, and she doesn't *jump*, exactly, but steps, like that, *plunk*

over the edge into the dark, her boyfriend keeps aiming for the small
lights across the water, she gets back in the boat, cold, small seal.

Radio Tuning

Does the old woman yelling
at her grandchildren listen
to the radio? She is twice
their size and sits smoking
on the stoop when they're at school.
She is there for hours
until her daughter arrives
from work. The old woman
goes inside. The daughter
sits smoking on the stoop.
The grandmother does the dishes,
gravy boats, sauce pans,
salad bowls, soup spoons.
If she's like my mother,
she'll listen to country & western—
but it could be Mozart or Bluegrass.
It is months before Christmas
lights go up in rowhouse
windows, months before
I take the freeway home
for Chanukah with my father
and stepmother, light the menorah
against the darkness,
remember how the temple fell,
and how we barely found the flame
amidst the rubble.
I think of holiness—
my mother must be at peace
at last, no children
or children's children breaking
through the dishes, the radio.
She wanted *communion,*
ascension, grace, forgiveness,
words I want to use myself, alone.

She heard *diaspora, scapegoat,*
never forget, holocaust,
vigilance, scribe, law,
history. My mother
hums along, ascends,
reveals herself beside a radio
with hands hot in dishwater.
I maintain my words:
old woman, dishwater, stoop,
yell, sacred, survival,
I write this vigil,
I do not forget.

New Elements

Old Jewish cemetery, Prague—for lack of space, this cemetery has twelve layers of burials; with each successive layer, the gravestones have been moved to the new layer of soil. The synagogue beside the cemetery has been turned into a memorial for Jewish victims of the Holocaust, with tens of thousands of Czech names printed on the interior walls. The site is visited by hundreds of tourists each day.

Why not start with the dead
layers, their stones pushed up
like tongues tasting the air
of two halves of the century?
They are bringing news
to their damp apartments,
they are banging brooms on the ceiling
of loud neighbors arguing late
ideas of new forms of darkness.
The kabbalists are testing relativity
against their charts of an endless alphabet,
they are breathing the faint residue
of new arrivals to the periodic table,
rearranging their circular formulae
accordingly.

In Pinkas synagogue, beside the stones,
the walls of names have been speaking
for years, learning language without bodies.
It takes time for their sounds
to travel the short space
to the tongues leaning on each other
in the soft grass, like stars
gone out centuries ago
whose light makes shadows
during nights of a thin moon.

The dead in their apartments listen.
They murmur among themselves, they exclaim
back and forth various ways
to explain to the names their meaning.
They are no squabbling crowd of pressed bones.
They say, *We will birth the future in your name.*
They say, *We will give you our God in your abandonment.*
They say, *We will continue with our work.*
Each name the name of God.
Each letter the wind of the Lord.
Each bone the balance of the Everlasting.
Each particle of dirt the Almighty.

Tattoo

All night rain made its bells on the streets,
people tossed under sheets washed in fanned air and murmuring
    televisons,
the broken fountains of Patterson Park filled up from the sky.

I was awake thinking of staying here.
I imagine my body has its reasons for cohesion,
my mind, its will for veins cushioned by the same skin
as always, like Baltimore spinning its tattoo,
sharp pricks of dark and light, in flowering tracks:

The searchlight of morning, white in rainwater's hovering steam,
sparks bottlecaps and safety glass tamped into the street,
casts shadows chasing old women's brooms on their marble steps.
On Lombard the Polish marquee exclaims another musical.
Flooded markets hawk fishermen's jewels on ice.
Roaches come like forest beetles on wet pavement
next to rainbows swirling on asphalt with its lifted gasoline,
a blue El Camino slicks by hauling a rebuilt black V-8 in back,
soft brick buildings look down from their measurable heights.

I open my door and this city could swallow me.
I open my door and this city could take me in.

Tree Heart

In a tree, blackbirds—a swarm, an open hive,
each black lightness its own small chamber:
The birds are not crows and are not death

and there are hundreds of them in the dryness,
quick late-summer breathing back at the leaves
they're hungry doubles of, wet shades of oxygen

gathering, a gather and a making of a flock
from a tree, a leaf a wing, two a bird, three a bird
with a beak and a flutter and a lack

of patience, sun up and a hot sheen
already, air heated and moving in quick drifts
shaking the leaves, the leaves are strange here,

so many of them shaking but still silent,
their sound is under the sound of the birds
loud in the light, light shooting clean

from one hillside through to the next, pale,
before it's gone and saturated everything,
light strung to a key the birds play, each of the hundred,

the birds are so loud it's easy to think this,
that the very light is sound:
Then one of them goes. No mission. No scout.

Just goes, comes back, like that, some more go
to land in the field below the tips of grain
so a haze begins, elastic, a stream of one body

from the tree like a cell's separation,
no flat, no hollow, no more,
you'd think, could fit where they all go

to eat, is all, all the flock's pieces
beating their wings for the ground.
It is almost. It is almost too much

for the field to carry where they've described
themselves, written their own low arcs,
rippling and settling for each new two or three

until the tree of birds is in the field. Murmuring.
The light is there. The light is a disappearance.
And they are eating. And they are making room.

Getting on a Horse

My mother is drawing a horse on the kitchen wall.
The horse is a gesture of a horse, drawn idly,
with scant, quick strokes of a bold pen or marker,
her left hand surer than her right, which cradles
the telephone, connecting her to someone
else, the horse a mind a mile away
dreaming of soft straw, light hooves, sweet apples.
Where *is* her mind, stroking the rough wood
paneling, boards really, nailed side by side
and stained dark—where is her mind
stroking the wood with her pen?
She is a girl drawing a horse.
After she leaves, the horse stays.
I stand in the kitchen
or walk through the door to the back yard,
I imagine her standing there,
I show my friends, I'm proud,
a horse, riderless, its owner away.

Rising

Once again I bang my head against Ecclesiastes.
James E. Reuter, my mother's father, who,
when his mind had just begun
to change, when I helped him first
from his chair, then from the dry bathtub
where he'd fallen, back to the toilet,
the smell of eighty-three years gusting
from under his shirt collar,
Now, he said, *you'll have a story
to tell your grandchildren—*
who, a year later, bed-bound,
awful nurse dismissed,
fearing the judgement of an Irish-Catholic
God and his own college-educated son,
fearing his life *vanity and a striving after wind,*
cried *I'm going to Hell! God dammit,
I'm going to go to Hell!* at daylight,
at starlight, at no one he knew:
he died as my future wife and I flew
for Europe. My mother's letter, the news,
descriptions of the funeral, relatives I'd yet to meet,
a packet of writings—*doggerel,*
he called it, and stories, and an essay,
an unfinished, terrifying page
he called "The Aging Process"—
those words were on our table when the cab
returned us home. What I see now,
looking in that flight to Europe—
two fiancees leaning heads to shoulders,
dreaming of bodies
in sickness and in health, success and failure—
what I'll always see, is the spirit of my grandfather
rising through the plane:
emerging from the Atlantic's darkness,

pausing a moment in the cabin's pressure,
his lost self beside his peace,
both pushed to the metal surrounding us
as we fly on to Frankfurt,
new Frankfurt, the few old buildings left
like rare stubble, where the good ghosts of citizens
and Jews pray for each old body,
letters pieced into words, to stories
rubbing like sea stones, like light,
among exacting conduits under cranes
lifting welders to skeletal I-beams,
the earth falling beneath the sun,
the plane's wings impossibly
keeping the fuselage from toppling,
all three of us flying,
how remarkable, how heavy it is.

Wild Flies

Above the dirt are big bugs flying.
The dirt makes dust on the dark stones,
changing them to a softer color.
Some bugs are gold, some are dragonflies,
and the bugs that fall over each other
in the air are wild flies.
He wants to be under the wild flies
and makes more dust with hand pats
until his hands are like the soft stones,
until he smells what the crawling bugs
smell and he lives in the small
crevices under wild flies and huge
green gliders making safety like the moon.
The sun is yellow but the sky is blue.
Sometimes he wishes he were blind,
by an accident, fireworks maybe,
so he could learn everything again
and tell people to leave him alone.
Sometimes his house is cold,
and sometimes it is dark.
Once he took a piss bath
in the bathtub, on his back
so the piss could go all over.
He knows it means something else.
Once he tried his hand
under hot water at the sink,
holding it until the burn feel,
then past the burn.
Piss doesn't burn. Piss is sweet.
Twice the dirt gets too bright
and when he closes his eyes,
he's in a red place with a million
sparkles, where he knows everyone lives.
The piss was warm and then it was cold

and he could make it warm again.
His hand is under dirt and under rocks
he's piled up for dragonflies,
his hand slid on his stomach
and the smell, the smell was sweet
and over him. He wanted more.
He knows that everyone forgets,
that he already can't remember
what he knows. His hand is pressure
and the wild flies are over him.

The Crowd

30th Street Station dwarfs the immense,
angular weight of the bronze-draped

statue of St. Christopher inside it.
The pigeons, *rats of the air*,

twisting through, don't need to beg
and aren't scared. They don't even see us.

They live in secret speech
of garbage and hunger, perch,

flutter up only when faced with an arm
raised sideways, winglike and sudden.

One, though, dirty and ragged from air
and waste on which the others thrive,

lives with us, limps tilting for us,
supplicant and monstrous as a storm

in the wrong season. It wants
what everybody wants. Everybody hates it.

It turns and rises up, knees locked,
spine stiff, wanting flight,

to burst, through shards of pecked glass
sucked hovering outside the atrium,

through need, purpose, through bodies and trouble,
the wanting a question, begging to be made flesh.

Collapsing Frame

How the scribe stays driven to his task,
    his puncture of a brow above the flat,
    the expansion. How I could be wrong.

Not to the swift, the quick, not now to little finches
    with their sudden meaning, a flourish, a bees' nest
    or nest of snakes, to maggots—

how I, a child, quiet, stared at the white roil
    in a stiff dog's head
    breathing alley waste, time, the record. And kept the quiet.

What changes to stay the same, where at six, decided,
    I would stand naked in the back doorway
    to become the doorframe and shade of oaks, cusping,

knowing it, skin cells drifting off as in a bath,
    air lifting goose bumps,
    without language, there, without a difference. Trying to.

What then the collapsed figure, grandfather, struck and slurred
    cursing *God dammit. God dammit.* his own body
    yet unscattered, whose eyes accuse his life in its last hour

without a God? He believed he'd never risen to his height
    and had read about the worst, most painful and exact,
    tortures reserved for those who stay in shadows

on the safest path—that, therefore, he would never now rise,
    that his unbelieving end, stranger to him
    and more terrible than any tragedy in Greek, would never
    end.

His troubled daughter, returned to take her station,
    lends a cool left hand to his forehead,
    saying every heart's at peace with his, calming him.

He knows her now for these cradled minutes. Rain, tinkling
    like a string of glass too tight, or voices held
    an octave higher, for an instant, than ears can register in time

to hear them falling, freights the window with its earthbound drive.
    Then the final exhalation, and the eyes—
    Staring? Fluttering? Looking still at a life found wanting?

For him, I don't believe it. How could all of someone's love be mediocre?
    How could my mother have the grace to tell me,
    Well—death is very final. And my father was my teacher.

Poppies in Provence

My mother sees fire, bright red
on top of a gentle hill, dripping

in little splotches down the lush
slope. The day is calm

and she is home between flames,
between poppies she paints as a low

volcano, a breast burning
with blood, a burning bush

with roots coming up like blackberries.
And if a burning bush, what instruction

does she hear, what voice
telling what she must do?

She paints herself into it, lounging
on one elbow, looking up

to the horizon not with longing
but with balance at the pale house

in the woods edging the hill,
the tan roof a wan nipple

nestled in evergreens and oaks.
And if the poppies are a breast

so full it's on fire, who
drinks flaming milk

on a hill in France?
Who could stand it?

Insulin

In a restaurant courtyard I saw a woman speaking with her date.
Her hands, close to each other to keep the jacket on her shoulders
from falling off, fluttered as she spoke
so that at times her fingers flicked a little riff
and at other times a whole hand pushed forward from her slowly.
Her yellow hair shone and I tried to figure the couple out,
how long they'd been together or a first date, what sort of people
they were and made themselves part of, if he thought her black
    pocketbook
was glamorous with its lacquered brass catch or sort of trashy,
if to her his smile was glib or really charming.
After a while they leaned toward each other for a moment,
he got up and walked between tables to the back,
she leaned her head to watch him, then reached toward her purse.
I wondered if she'd get out lipstick, maybe, and a little mirror,
and maybe she'd look past it, our eyes would meet
then look away, a little restaurant thing we'd share.
What she got out was a needle, held it to the light and shrugged her
    jacket off
so her hair cut down across the angles of her black vest.
She swept the needle towards the arm held against her leg,
hair a curtain to shield her, a cape that part of her became
so that the push was hidden, the needle, the insulin emptying in.
It was like freeing a jar with a sharp tap and one twist—
the grace of it turned my thoughts into cheap speculations,
turned me clumsy, sitting there with my hands in my lap.

At a Window, Wide to September

Late sun illuminates benign insects
making slow chaos, a hover, a spin, a brief

flotilla above the lilacs, above the two aspen
we planted, their thin forms without hips,

their leaves rattling like early dry tongues.
In fact, I have no idea if the insects are benign.

Two weeks ago we talked as plainly as the low
sun making the bugs visible, giving them their sultry

glow. We spoke without rancor or our customary
weapons. We spoke knowing we would leave

each other. Now my hands are in my lap, our hearts
dirt and stone and small animals in our chests.

End of May, Leaving

All the old stories about loss
aren't true. Fields of dead poppies

aren't dead until after their sticky
milk oozes from neat razor slits.

And anyway their seeds make new
flowers with the same red

paper-thin astonishment each year.
The stories about loss are a myth.

It's true myths are about loss, but think
of Persephone snatched in the warm field.

Persephone went into the earth.
She could have become simply wiser

rather than living half each year
in the netherworld because she ate

six pomegranate seeds.
We learn our lives hinge

on hunger and things in plain view.
This table I'm leaning on will not

go away, the chair beneath me
I'll take, the old nickel gooseneck

lamp will illuminate a new corner,
the enamel single-drawer phone table

will have a new phone, my fingers
after waking from dreams of a split earth

and scarlet seeds will be my fingers
holding the coffee cup in the morning.

June, a New House

Every story about loss is true.
There is anger and confusion

and terrible clarity when, falling asleep alone,
I feel her head push at my neck, my hand

in the valley of her waist, naked, naked, for solace
in my dreams. And what do I dream?

Of orange flowers she leaves at my doorstep.
Of violence in our bed, of kisses

we have kept to ourselves, food
shoved in my mouth I can't swallow.

The birds have been waking me, early.
The air is fine, a little blurry.

July, Hungry

The thing about loss
is that it's not always around.

Loss is a cat, trawling
all night for neighborhood mice, shadows

in intricate shapes it wants us
with it to leap and lock our teeth into.

We call out for loss, we wonder
where it's gone. In the morning

it scratches at the door, mewling,
hungry. I open to the sound,

feed it. At night, if I forget,
I might later wake in the quiet,

hungry, sternum a black weight,
thin starlight penciling the dark edges

of the kitchen, hush, clink of a spoon,
bare body fleshing the room, warm.

Fireworks

Down the block, kids dart
to the intersection to light their fireworks.
Trees canopy the street, smoke drifts low
towards us. We time our shooting sparks
to overlap, asphalt blooms flaring in the haze:
I'm with three couples, turning our faces
to the sky when expanding spheres,
like effervescent garlic stalks, bloom
above rooftops from church parking lots.
Our chests feel booms from downtown
river barges' professional displays.
When our own fireworks—Mini Monsters,
a Giant Fountain, a Pinwheel—surprise us
with last cracklings of sparks skittering,
hopping hard against the street, we laugh,
we clap our hands. We each take sparklers,
wave arcs, loops, curls of flaring light
above our heads, across our bodies,
doing little dances in the sputtering haze.

Driving home, late, past flares
between parked cars, high sparkles
hovering above a rooftop, teenagers
loosely bicycling to a fresh neighborhood,
bits of paper and grey powder marking launch pads
on humped intersections, on sidewalks and driveways—
there's a night chill, my windows are rolled up,
the heat is kicking in. I miss the first turn
across town, instead take the broad street
past the house where my wife and I lived
for five years, then a mile later feel the steering wheel
pull towards our newer house I'd moved from.
I tell myself *go steady, drive on,* and I do.

Two months ago, dozing close to midnight,
I'm waiting for my wife, who's out for beers
with colleagues after a six-day project.
She gets home, happy, and sleepily I tell her
how I'd spent some time angry
for how late it was without her home.
Suddenly we're in a tantrum, tossing flares,
igniting flashes, shooting sharp hisses past
our ears, sending sparks scuttling from one room
to the next, booming hearts dry into our mouths,
downstairs, upstairs, not taking turns, until she's up
in the bedroom, I'm down, I think it's over
but I spark again, pound upstairs, reach
the threshold of our room, punch hard
the half-open door with a right jab from my shoulder,
stand there shaking in the round silence.

My wife is calm on the bed as I hit
the door and lob a last explosion.
She stays prone, arms straight beside her
and her legs, together but not touching, unbent.
Her head faces towards the ceiling, her still
mouth and eyes an anchor from which she looks
not at me, not at me, not glazed, clearly up.
I go back down and feel awful, try to salvage
one bit of pride from a mangled review
of what I've done. I sit in the downstairs room
where I've been sleeping, stare dumbly at the dark
television, back to the closed door—does it matter
what we said? Are there any grownup words?

Younger, twenty-three, not yet married,
we went to Planned Parenthood.
She's been sick in the mornings, but we know
it isn't the right time, we're young,
we don't know our future.
I'm sitting in the waiting room, surprised
at the cheery magazines, when my wife's name

is called and she stands, I stand, she walks over
to the door. Across the carpet, she turns,
smiles and winks at me, for me, for us both,
a gift I'll turn and study every year, she winks
before she turns and goes into the room.
Time had no limits then, anything that happened
once, was proof we could have it again.
Now she knocks on my door downstairs,
comes in and sits beside me, says
I don't want us fighting, can I sleep here,
it's all I know right now to do.
We lie beside each other, drift into our sleep,
warm under covers, hands on the small
of each other's back, she's over there,
through smoke, waving sparklers in each hand,
turning designs, she's winking, she's beautiful.

Dirt Heart

Sometimes there is a shape to them,
the blackbirds—an arc or swirl, a wave,

the air like water following
itself around a rock.

And sometimes the air bursts
with the black specks

suddenly like fall leaves
gusted ahead of storm clouds

before the rain has come
to batter them out of the sky,

a great crowd of leaves
like a startled flock before it's a shape.

The road goes down to the river
and the crowd is there, a startle

low across the dirt, the air full with it,
almost swollen, so large, right there,

as if the sky were in front of your face,
something to rush towards and be in it,

like a building half demolished
before an excavation for a new one,

when its exposed rooms and hallways,
its floors with wall-to-wall carpet

dripping from a lip jumbled with plumbing
and chunks of concrete hanging on rebar,

make it more present, these fleshy cavities,
than in its life of still composure:

to be in it, eye mesmerized,
no scale anymore, to rush in

and through it, this bird one way,
that one another, all of them

a tumbling swarm from one side
of the road to the other

before they're a flock and turn
their wingtips thin to the horizon

so for a moment disappear,
then settle into the field.

The dirt at the field's edge is dry, and light.
Tiny stones float on the fine layer.

It's soft and in the shade it's cool,
in the sun it's hot to the hand.

Here where the blackbirds have added
and taken, where the fingers press

they stay before the wind,
the heel, the palm and what it's held,

the hand can lift and leave itself,
its fingers filled with air,

here where the birds have passed.
Where the body has just come back.

Where the blackbirds have
broken and made their shape.

The interior text and display type and back cover were set in Adobe Jenson, a faithful electronic version of the 1470 roman face of Nicolas Jenson. Jenson was a Frenchman employed as the mintmaster at Tours. Legend has it that he was sent to Mainz in 1458 by Charles VII to learn the new art of printing in the shop of Gutenberg, and import it to France. But he never returned, appearing in Venice in 1468; there his first roman types appeared, in his edition of Eusebius. He moved to Rome at the invitation of Pope Sixtus IV, where he died in 1480.

Type historian Daniel Berkeley Updike praises the Jenson Roman for "its readability, its mellowness of form, and the evenness of color in mass." Updike concludes, "Jenson's roman types have been the accepted models for roman letters ever since he made them, and, repeatedly copied in our own day, have never been equalled."

The front cover typeface is Interstate. Designed by Tobias Frere-Jones in the period 1993–1999, Interstate is closely related to the FHWA Series fonts, a signage alphabet drawn for the United States Federal Highway Administration in 1949. While optimal for signage, Interstate has refinements making it suitable for text setting in print and on-screen, and gained popularity as such in the 1990s. Due to its wide spacing, it is best suited for display usage in print.

Silverfish Review Press is committed to preserving ancient forests and natural resources. We elected to print *Bastard Heart* on 30% post consumer recycled paper, processed chlorine free. As a result, for this printing, we have saved: 1 tree (40' tall and 6-8" diameter), 499 gallons of water, 293 kilowatt hours of electricity, 64 pounds of solid waste, and 120 pounds of greenhouse gases. Thomson-Shore, Inc. is a member of Green Press Initiative, a nonprofit program dedicated to supporting authors, publishers, and suppliers in their efforts to reduce their use of fiber obtained from endangered forests. For more information, visit www.greenpressinitiative.org.

Cover design by Valerie Brewster, Scribe Typography.
Text design by Rodger Moody and Connie Kudura, ProtoType Graphics.
Printed on acid-free papers and bound by Thomson-Shore, Inc.